GW00858887

The

and
Miss Minkin

by

Sandra Horn

with illustrations by

Katie Stewart

Cat Tales from an old Sussex farmhouse

The Clucket Press

To all the dear folk who share

memories of the real 'Ghyllside Farm',

with my love

Text copyright © 2012 Sandra Horn
www.tattybogle.co.uk

Cover and illustrations copyright © 2015 Katie Stewart,
www.magicowldesign.com

Stories 1,2, 5 and 6 were first published in Great Britain in 1999 by
Hodder Children's Books

This edition published 2016
by
The Clucket Press, 220 Hill Lane
Southampton, SO15 7NR

All rights reserved. No part of this publication may be reproduced or transmitted in any form or by any means, electronic or mechanical, including photocopying, recording or any information storage or retrieval system, without prior permission in writing from the publishers.

The right of Sandra Horn to be identified as the author of this Work and the right of Katie Stewart to be identified as the designer of this work, has been asserted by them in accordance with the Copyright, Designs and Patents Act 1988.

ISBN-13: 978-1-909568-08-2

Layout and setting by Niall Horn

Contents

The Naming Song

1: The Naming Song

Hob lived under the hearthstone at Ghyllside Farm, but no-one had ever seen him except Miss Minkin the tabby cat. The farmhouse was very old, and Hob had been there for more years than he could count, although he remembered talk of Good Queen Bess, and Henry the Something, and beacons being set along the Sussex coast in case the French invaded.

In the days long ago, if one of the housemaids had been extra kind and good about her work, Hob would put a silver sixpence in her shoe. If she had been bad and grumpy, he would tie her apron-strings in a tangle. Now that there were no maids and no sixpences at Ghyllside Farm, he didn't get up to many tricks at all.

At night, when the farmer and his wife and their children were asleep in bed, Hob liked to come up into the kitchen and tell yarns by the fire with Miss Minkin. They had been friends since she was a small kitten. They shared the dish of cream that Jenny the farmer's wife put out each night, and talked about the days gone by. In the morning, before the sun came up, Hob slipped back under the hearthstone and Miss Minkin took a little nap until breakfast time.

Miss Minkin was very fussy about her appearance. She washed and smoothed her beautiful fur several times a day.

'I like to be clean,' said Miss Minkin.

Jenny the farmer's wife liked to be clean too. She kept the house neat and tidy all year round, but every Spring she went cleaning mad. She tidied, dusted, polished and scrubbed the house from attics to cellars and there was nothing anybody could do about it. It was all most upsetting to Miss Minkin's nerves.

• • •

Early one Spring morning, Miss Minkin was dozing by the hearth when Jenny flew downstairs with her arms full of dusters, mops and polishing cloths. Miss Minkin waited for Jenny to bring her breakfast, but no breakfast came. When she meowed very loudly to remind Jenny about it, Jenny only said,

'I'm too busy spring cleaning to think about anything else. Why don't you fend for yourself? Go and catch something.'

Miss Minkin could hardly believe her ears. She did not want to go and catch something! She wanted her dish of nice white fish with all the bones taken out. She sat up very straight in the middle of the kitchen, with her back to Jenny, and thrashed her tail from side to side.

'Oh, all right then!' said Jenny, 'but you can have it outside in the yard so you're not under my feet.'

'Under her feet indeed! How very rude!' said Miss Minkin under her breath.

She would like to have stalked off with her tail in the air and not come back until Jenny thought she was lost forever, and then she'd be sorry, but she was hungry. She ate all the fish first and then stalked off.

In the evening, when the house was quiet, Miss Minkin slipped back through the catflap into the kitchen, and hoped that Hob would appear soon from under the hearthstone. She wanted to tell him what a dreadful day she'd had, and how nobody had nice manners any more. But what was this? The fire was out! The hearth was swept clean and in the grate was a heap of crinkly red paper instead of warm glowing coal.

'This,' said Miss Minkin, 'is the giddy limit.'

'What is?' asked Hob, appearing from the shadows, 'I see the fire-irons have been polished. Shine up nice, don't they? And the fire's been let out. It must be Spring. I thought there was something in the air. Old Mother Mouse has built a nest under the wash house floor and she's got a nice little brood in there – must be seven or eight mousekins.'

Miss Minkin pricked up her ears.

'Oh really?' she said, licking her lips and looking thoughtful.

Hob got out his pipe.

'That's a good dish of cream,' he said. The dish was brim-full.

'I expect it's Jenny's way of making up for being so unkind,' said Miss Minkin, 'and I forgive her, but the hearthstone is cold with the fire out and I'm not very comfortable. I do not like Spring. It's too much disturbance.'

Hob scratched his head.

'We could sit in the fireplace, on the crinkly paper,' he suggested, 'it might be quite cosy. What do you think, my dear? I'll bring the cream.'

Miss Minkin said she would try it, although it wasn't what she was used to. She climbed into the fireplace and kneaded the paper with her paws into a soft red nest. Hob said it was better than a cushion.

He looked up the chimney. 'See up yonder,' he said.

There above them was a sickle moon and a single bright star.

'Beautiful!' purred Miss Minkin. 'Shall we serenade, it, my dear?'

Hob got out his fiddle, Miss Minkin cleared her throat, and they sang a couple of verses of 'O Silver Moon' before getting down to the cream.

Miss Minkin said it was a happy ending to a very trying day.

• • •

Next morning, Jenny was still cleaning and turning out cupboards, but she did remember Miss Minkin's breakfast. After she had finished and washed her face, Miss Minkin curled up in the airing cupboard among the soft blankets for a morning nap, but she was soon turned out again by Jenny.

'Sheer madness!' muttered Miss Minkin, 'taking everything out and putting it back in again! She should see the vet and get something for her nerves, in my opinion.'

Unfortunately, no-one was listening.

...

Miss Minkin left the racketty house and went to the barn, thinking she would have her snooze in the hay, but what did she see? Her own special hole in the bottom of the door was covered up with a piece of wood. She could hear some very interesting noises from inside the barn: 'cheep! cheep! cheep!' She pushed at the wood with her paw.

'Oi!' shouted the farmer, 'you keep away from there, pussy! There's newly-hatched chicks in there!'

Miss Minkin put her head on one side, as if to say, 'oh purrlease! I only want to play Chase and Pounce with them.'

'SCAT!!' shouted the farmer, very loud and cross.

Miss Minkin left, hurriedly. She spent the day in the woodpile, which was rather damp and cobwebby.

That evening, when the house was quiet and everyone had gone to bed, Hob and Miss Minkin met on the hearth as usual. There was still no fire, but Miss Minkin said she was getting used to it. Hob was in a dancing mood, so they danced a gavotte on the hearthstone before climbing into the fireplace with the dish of cream. They were almost at the last drop when there was a scuffling noise above them and a lump of soot dropped into the dish. Miss Minkin declared she would not touch another morsel now, but Hob didn't mind a drop of good honest dirt, so he scraped out the dish. Then there was a scratching noise, and more soot fell. Hob looked up the chimney. Instead of a moon in a dark blue sky, he saw a mass of twigs.

'Oh ho!' he said, 'bird's nest!'

Miss Minkin pricked up her ears.

'How lovely!' she said, 'The moon is all very pretty, but it cannot compare with a nest full of dear little baby birds – and so convenient, too!'

Hob looked gloomy.

'That's all very well, my dear, but we won't be sitting here in comfort any more. All sorts of rubbish will fall on us, and the chimney will be blocked, so when they come to light the fire again, there'll be nothing but soot and smoke and maybe the chimney afire.'

Miss Minkin was about to say that Hob was making a fuss about nothing when a very large lump of soot fell on her left front paw and made her beautiful fur all black. She looked up. A rotten dusty twig came clattering down and landed right on her pink nose. Miss Minkin sneezed and said, 'Yow!' She bared her teeth and glared up the chimney. The mother bird was looking down just then and saw a pair of fierce green eyes and two rows of sharp teeth below. She didn't like it.

'Bert, we'll have to move!' she called to her husband, 'I don't like it here. I want a nest in a tree, like everybody else.'

Her husband, who had been flying backwards and forwards with twigs all day until he was giddy, said, 'Nonsense! You'll soon get used to it – and it's a very smart address.'

Miss Minkin frowned. She had changed her mind about the bird's nest.

'Bother! They are going to stay,' she said, 'and we'll have to sit on the cold hearth or be showered with nasty rubbish every night.'

Hob said nothing. He winked at Miss Minkin, then got out his pipe and lit it. He huffed and puffed, then began to blow smoke-rings, one after the other. The smoke-rings drifted up the chimney until they reached the nest. The mother bird gave an angry squawk, then a cough.

'Fire!' she shouted. 'You and your smart address, Bert Bird! We'll all be choked with smoke and fried to a crisp!'‘Oh, all right then!' said her husband, ‘We'll move. How was I to know that they'd light a fire at this time of year? Come on, we'll spend the night in the barn and tomorrow we'll find somewhere else.'

‘In a TREE next time!' said his wife, and they flew away together, quarrelling as they went.

‘Oh, well done my dear!' purred Miss Minkin.

‘It was nothing,' said Hob. Then he waved his pipe three times round and said ‘Begone!' up the chimney. The twigs hopped off the chimney pot and rolled into the gutter.

‘Lovely view of the moon!' said Miss Minkin.

They settled down on the crinkly paper, and Miss Minkin washed the soot off her paw while Hob played a soft lilting tune on his fiddle.

‘Peace at last,' purred Miss Minkin.

• • •

When the tune had ended and the kitchen fell quiet, Miss Minkin thought she would go on with her nice little wash. Halfway through, she stopped quite suddenly with one paw in the air, and swivelled her ears.

‘What's that?' she said, ‘There's someone about in the yard. I thought they were all abed.'

Hob swivelled his ears too. 'It's coming from the stable,' he said, 'something must be wrong out there. Come on.'

They slipped out of the cat flap. The stable was across the yard, and although it was dark, the door was open a little way and a shaft of yellow light lay across the ground like a path.

'Wait!' hissed Miss Minkin, 'There's someone there! They might see you!'

'Not a chance!' said Hob, 'don't you worry.'

Hob and Miss Minkin followed the bright path across the cobbles and crept quietly into the stable. They stood in the shadows by the wall. Nobody saw them, and nobody heard. Jenny and her husband were trying to soothe a fretful mare, who was lying on the straw.

'She's having a foal,' whispered Miss Minkin, 'at teatime Jenny said she was taking her time about it.'

By and by, they saw a leggy chestnut foal being born.

Jenny said, 'she'll be all right now. It's been a long labour, and she's worn out.'

'Me too,' yawned her husband, 'let's go and get some sleep.'

Hob and Miss Minkin drew back deeper into the shadows. Hob tugged his beard three times, and although Jenny and her husband passed close by, they saw nothing but two withered turnips in the hay as they went out. The two withered turnips shook themselves, and anyone could see that they were really a tabby cat and a Hob. They came out of the shadows and crept up to the stall. The mare was deep asleep and the little foal by her side was still and silent. His eyes were open, but he was not looking at anything.

'I don't like the look of him,' said Hob. He walked up to the foal and said, 'Hello, little fellow.'

The foal did not move. Hob waved his hand close to the foal's eyes. He did not blink or stir.

'Whatever is the matter with him?' asked Miss Minkin.

Hob scratched his head.

'I think he hasn't been sung his naming song, so he can't start being a horse yet,' he said, 'his mother must have fallen asleep before she could sing it. Let's try to wake her up.'

Hob and Miss Minkin did their best. They patted the mare's face. They said 'Hello!' very loud. They shouted and sang in her ear. She was far too tired to wake up.

‘There’s nothing else for it,’ said Hob, ‘WE’LL have to horse him, or he won’t know who he is.’

‘Mother cats name their kittens too,’ said Miss Minkin, ‘shall I sing their special song to him? It’s about beautiful green eyes and sleek fur, sharp teeth and claws, pink tongues lapping milk, mousing and bird-catching…’

‘I don’t think that would do at all, I’m afraid, my dear,’ said Hob, ‘I’ll have to try and remember the horse song. My second cousin Fergal sang it to me once, but it was a long time ago and in Erse, of course. Hmm.’

Hob paced round in the straw muttering to himself, but every time he thought he’d remembered a bit of the song, there was a noise and it muddled him up. A bat scrabbled in the eaves, a mouse squeaked, a rat rustled in the straw, a moth blundered round the lamp.

‘This is hopeless!’ he said.

Miss Minkin said she would fix it. She crouched like a tiger at the entrance to the stall and glared round the stable with her big green eyes. Then she began to growl, very low but very fierce.

All the scurrying creatures in the stable stood still for a second, then dived for holes and burrows and perches and kept perfectly quiet until morning.

'Thank you, my dear,' said Hob, and he began to pace and mutter once more. Finally, he said, 'I think I've got it!'

Hob walked up close to the little foal's ear, cleared his throat, and sang the horse-naming song. It had a strange-sounding tune like nothing Miss Minkin had ever heard before.

It began with the shadow-black horses who pull the silver chariot of the moon across the sky, and as Hob sang the stable seemed to fill with the winds of sleep and stars thrown off by sparking hooves.

Miss Minkin saw the little horse's left ear twitch.

Then Hob sang about the golden steeds of the sun, scattering light from their streaming manes as they fly from the farthest East to the uttermost West.

The little horse twitched his right ear.

Miss Minkin held her breath.

The song went on to tell of the foam-white storm horses of the sea, with lightning in their eyes and thunder in their galloping hooves.

The little horse twitched both ears.

'Oh, bravo!' murmured Miss Minkin.

Hob was nearly at full pitch now, singing about carousel horses with golden manes and scarlet saddles, hobby horses with bells on their bridles, and rocking horses galloping across the floor to a magical land far away.

The little horse lifted his head.

Miss Minkin sighed.

'Last of all and best of all,' sang Hob, 'are the horses of the earth; the sure-footed children of the South Wind. Once upon a day, the wind caught up handfuls of earth from all places and all seasons, and he breathed on them. He breathed the black frosts and white snows of winter, the cloud-dappled ground of spring, the gold of ripe summer wheat and the silky autumn brown of chestnuts.'

Miss Minkin could smell sweet meadow-grass as the song went on, and hear hooves and swishing tails under a wide sky.

The song ended with, 'The South Wind breathed beauty and strength, speed and gentleness into them, and he named them Horse. You are a horse! Wake up and be!'

The little horse blinked, as if he could see something at last. He made a soft whinnying sound. All at once, his mother woke up, although it was only a very small whinny, and she snuggled close to him and whinnied back.

Miss Minkin wiped a tear from her eye. Hob and the mare looked at each other.

'It's all right,' said Hob, 'he's horsed.' The mare nodded her head.

'Come on,' said Hob to Miss Minkin, 'let's be getting home-along. There's nothing more for us to do here.'

They stepped through the stable door as the first light of a new spring day was silvering the Downs and the birds were waking up, and they stopped for a moment to breathe the morning air.

'Primroses will soon be opening on the ghyll bank,' said Hob.

'Yes,' purred Miss Minkin, 'It's a lovely time of year.'

Then they slipped in through the catflap as quietly as shadows.

The Empty Dish

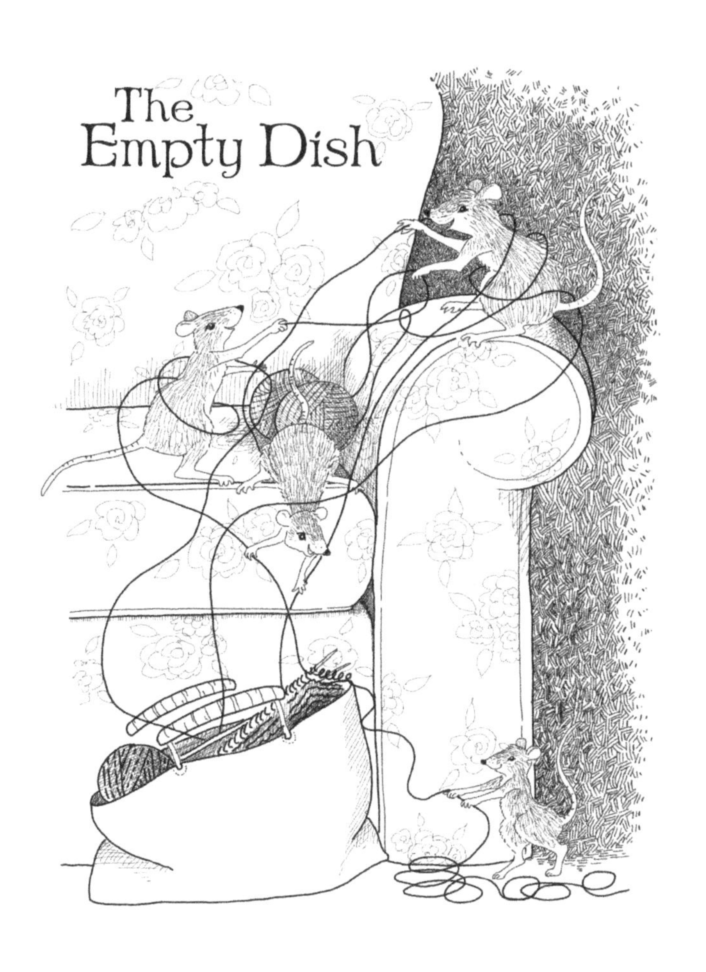

2: The Empty Dish

One drowsy May night, when the stars were bright and a big yellow moon shone full in through the kitchen window, Hob was in the mood for storytelling. He told tale after tale of the little folk and the magic and mischief they made, long years ago. Once upon a time, he had seen the fairy queen riding a white horse no bigger than a beetle. Miss Minkin was very interested to hear about it. Then Miss Minkin remembered a story about her great great-uncle Arthur, a famous ginger ratter, who met the king of the elves by moonlight and was put under a spell. He was never the same after that. He took to sitting on the chimney pot and quacking like a Barbary duck. Hob said it must have been mighty strong magic. There wasn't much of it about nowadays.

...

They talked until the moon slipped down behind the hill and the stars faded away. The summer night was warm, and the kitchen was very snug.

Hob's head began to nod. Miss Minkin yawned, very wide and pink. They shared the last few drops of cream in the bottom of the dish, and then they fell asleep side by side on the hearth. By and by, the mice came peeping round the door, but no-one pulled a face or said 'PSSSTT!' so they crept into the kitchen. Hob and Miss Minkin were snoring by the embers and dreaming of the good old days. The mice made themselves at home and had a high old time. They ran up the tablecloth and bit all the apples in the bowl. They rolled a candle-end onto the floor and took it away. They tossed Jenny's knitting around until it was all dropped stitches and tangle. They got in the cupboard and danced on the butter. They nibbled the bacon set out for breakfast. Hob and Miss Minkin slept sound, while the mice made all the mischief they could think of.

When Jenny came downstairs in the morning, the mice had run away and Miss Minkin was still deep asleep. Jenny rattled the latch on the kitchen door, and Hob woke up and slipped away under the hearthstone as quick as could be. Jenny looked round the kitchen at all the mess and muddle and she gave a great shriek.

'Lawks-a-mussy! What ever's been in here? The bacon is eat and the butter is spoiled and my knitting's all in a muddle. It's they wicked little mice, I'll be bound. Miss Minkin, what were you a-thinking of, you lazy creature?'

Miss Minkin woke up with a start and twitched her ears. She was in deep disgrace.

Jenny was grumpy all day long, even when Miss Minkin purred and rubbed her beautiful head round Jenny's legs.

'You won't get round me like that, you naughty puss!' she said.

Miss Minkin went and sat behind the sofa.

When bedtime came, she purred again very sweetly, but Jenny did not fetch the cream jug. Instead, she said, 'No cream for you, Miss Minkin!' You are too well fed and it has made you idle. You must learn better, and keep the mice out of the kitchen!'

Then she stumped off to bed, leaving the dish empty. Miss Minkin could not believe ears and eyes. She looked long and hard at the dish. Then she sniffed it. Then she licked it. There was not the smallest drop of cream in it anywhere.

'Yow-ow-ow!' cried Miss Minkin.

When Hob came up for his visit, Miss Minkin told him that she was in disgrace because of the wicked little mice, and there was no cream. He and Miss Minkin looked at the empty dish for a long time and felt very sad. They were too upset to think of any stories.

Miss Minkin sighed, 'I do miss the cream.'

'So do I,' said Hob. He sighed even louder. His stomach began to grumble.

'No use moping,' he said, 'I'll fetch me fiddle and play us a merry tune.'

'That won't fill our bellies,' said Miss Minkin.

'No more will moping and mumping,' said Hob, 'so we might as well be cheerful.'

• • •

Hob tuned his fiddle and tightened the bow, then struck up with 'Bonny Sweet Robin' and Miss Minkin began to dance. First, she danced slow and stately and Hob kept time by tapping his foot. They still felt sad, and could still hear Hob's rumbly stomach. Hob played louder and faster and Miss Minkin twirled round like a spinning top. That was better! They cheered up a little, and soon they both began to sing. They sang loud and melodious. Up went Miss Minkin on the tips of her toes. Hob's elbow flew up and down. The song grew louder and louder. There was such a noise and such a jumping and capering that Hob forgot he was playing a reel and he slipped into some old fairy music instead. All of a sudden, the fire leapt into life. Flames and sparks shot up the chimney. The clock struck twenty-nine. The fire-irons jangled. Miss Minkin wobbled on top E like a siren. The sparrows under the eaves woke up with a fright.

'House a-fire! House a-fire!' they shrieked, 'Help! Help!! Help!!!'

•••

Jenny woke up. She jumped out of bed and came running downstairs with one slipper on. As she scrabbled at the door catch, Hob waved the fiddle bow three times round and said, 'Husha!' and everything fell as silent as stone. The birds went back to sleep. The fire died down to ashes. Hob slid into the shadows behind the coalbox, and Miss Minkin lay down and closed her eyes. Jenny flung open the door.

'Is there anybody there?' she said. She stepped inside. The kitchen was just as she had left it, with the dear old cat curled up on the hearth asleep.

'Miss Minkin!' Jenny called.

Miss Minkin opened one eye.

'Did you hear anything, my dear?' asked Jenny.

Miss Minkin opened the other eye.

'Meeeeeoh?'

Jenny looked all round the kitchen. She couldn't see anything that might have made such a noise. She shook her head and went back to bed.

'I'm sure I wasn't dreaming,' she said.

• • •

No sooner had she got back into bed than Hob came out from behind the coalbox. He tried to think of something cheerful, but the cream dish was still empty and so was his stomach. He sat down on the hearth with a sigh.

'We are getting sad again, my dear,' said Miss Minkin, 'let's be merry instead.'

'Right enough,' said Hob. He picked up his fiddle and he and Miss Minkin began to dance again.

'Not too fast nor yet too loud,' said Hob, 'we fetched the farmer's wife down last time.'

'Yes,' said Miss Minkin thoughtfully, 'So we did. Just play that last tune again, will you my dear? I did like it most particularly.'

Hob began to play the strange old tune.

'A little faster, please!' called Miss Minkin. She leaped over the fire-irons. Hob played like the wind. The wild music scampered all round the kitchen. The coal jumped up and down. The clock hopped along the mantelpiece. The sparrows in the eaves shrieked so loud that Rooster woke up in the yard and sounded his morning bugle-call,

'OOOOO-aah! OOOO-ah!! OOOOOO-ah!!!' even though it was only three o'clock.

That woke the dog, who began to jump around and bark, 'Burglars! Burglaaaars!'

Up out of bed got Jenny, and stumbled downstairs in a rush with no slippers on at all.

'Husha!' said Hob as he stepped behind the fire-irons out of sight. All the noises stopped.

Miss Minkin curled up quickly on the hearth and closed her eyes.

Jenny looked all round the silent kitchen. She scratched her head and blinked a sleepy eye.

'Did you hear anything, my dear?' she said.

Miss Minkin yawned very wide.

'Meeoh? Neeoh!' she said.

Jenny crouched down and looked under the table and the chairs. She picked up the sofa cushions and peered behind them. She even looked under the rug and behind the calendar on the wall. There was nothing to be found, so she shook her head and went grumbling and puzzled back to bed.

As soon as she was gone, Hob and his fiddle slid out of the shadows once more.

Hob looked towards the dish.

'Did she leave anything, my dear?' he asked.

'Not....yet,' said Miss Minkin, 'are you ready?'

•••

Hob and Miss Minkin began the wild ruckus again. Faster and faster went the dance. Miss Minkin leaped and twirled like a kitten. The music soared louder and louder. The fire-irons spun round in a perfect pirouette and the old sofa tapped its four fat feet. All the creatures in the house and yard woke up, even the bull in the barn.

'Muuuuuurder! Muuuuuurder!!' he roared.

He bellowed so loud, the clock fell off the mantelpiece with a clang and a clatter. Poor sleepy Jenny came clumping back downstairs with a headache and cold toes.

'Husha!' said Hob from behind the fire-irons, and all was silent and still once more.

'I can't stand this no longer!' bawled Jenny, 'if my husband wakes up he'll storm and shout and be in a rage. Are you sure you didn't hear anything?'

Miss Minkin did not answer.

'Were you a-sleeping?' asked Jenny.

Miss Minkin blinked twice and looked indignant. Jenny picked up the shattered clock.

'Miss Minkin hasn't been up on that mantelpiece for many a long year,' she said to herself, 'so how did my poor old clock get all broke to bits? It must be they dratted mice. That's all I can think.'

She bent down and stroked Miss Minkin's head.

'Will you stay awake and watch and frighten them away, my dear?'

Miss Minkin did not answer. She gazed sorrowfully at the empty cream dish and twitched her tabby tail.

'Please,' said Jenny.

Miss Minkin sniffed at the empty dish and gave Jenny a long green stare.

Jenny sighed, 'Oh, all right then,' and fetched the jug of cream. She filled the dish right up to the brim. Miss Minkin purred and rubbed her head on Jenny's leg.

'Good pussy,' said Jenny, and she went wearily back to bed.

...

Hob slid out of the shadows. He smiled when he saw the dish brimming with cream.

'How are you feeling now, my dear?' he asked.

'Much more cheerful, thank you,' said Miss Minkin, 'have you got your silver thimble with you?'

Hob pulled the thimble from his pocket and they drank their fill of the cool sweet cream.

Then Hob filled his pipe with baccy and whispered a tale of far away and long ago. Miss Minkin sang a nice quiet song her mother had taught her, about three little kittens who had lost their mittens. Hob said it was very sad and beautiful.

When the mice came creeping and peeped round the kitchen door, they both said 'PSSTTT!' very fiercely, and the mice took fright and ran away without doing any mischief.

Upstairs, out of sight and sound, Jenny and her husband slept and snored until the sun came up and Rooster crowed again.

Midsummer
Magic

3: Midsummer Magic

It was midsummer. The Downs were dusted with golden hay as the grass dried crisp in the long hot days. The ghyll had shrunk to a gnat-haunted trickle. Miss Minkin was worn out from stalking butterflies, who did not play fair and always flew away just as she pounced. She had retired to the scented shade of the rosemary bush and was dozing and dreaming. Her ears twitched and her tail lashed as the butterflies in her dream sailed across the garden, big as tablecloths, poking out their long curly tongues at her. Suddenly she was woken up by a loud clanking and clattering. The farmer had come into the garden carrying a large metal tub. He dropped it right down by Miss Minkin's bush.

'Come on out with that charcoal,' he shouted, 'or we'll be eating those sausages at midnight.'

Miss Minkin was very sensitive to noise. She did not like being disturbed. She got up and went indoors with her tail in the air. She sat by the hearth and washed her beautiful fur. In the evening, Miss Minkin waited and waited, but Hob did not come. She began to grow alarmed. Hob always came to see her, every evening, and he was never late. She went to his secret door behind the fire-irons and listened. She couldn't see anything because it was an invisible door, but she thought she heard a huffing and a puffing coming from somewhere. All of a sudden Hob sprang out in front of her.

'Yow!' squealed Miss Minkin. It gave her quite a nasty fright.

'Oof! Sorry my dear,' said Hob, 'my door spell is wearing off and I could hardly squeeze through tonight. I must make it again or I'll be stuck one side or the other. That won't do at all. If I'm 'tother side I won't be able to get out, and if I'm this side I won't be able to get back.'

Miss Minkin was much alarmed.

'Please fix it right away, my dear.'

'Ah, that's the trouble,' said Hob, 'I need to write the easing runes on the hinges again, they've almost rubbed away, and I can't.'

'Why not?'

'I haven't got anything to write them with. I had a bit of oaktree charcoal I used the first time, but

I trod on it, and it crumbled away to dust.' Miss Minkin put her head on one side and thought. Then she said, 'Try Jenny's pot.'

Hob raised his shaggy white eyebrows. 'How would that help?'

'It's her everything pot,' said Miss Minkin, 'I heard her husband say it had a little bit of the whole world in it, so it's bound to have some oaktree charcoal. It's on the mantelpiece.'

Hob looked up at the pot and waved his arms.

'Come!' he said. Jenny's pot hopped off the mantelpiece, sailed through the air and landed at Hob's feet.

'Oh bravo!' murmured Miss Minkin.

Hob tipped the pot upside-down and out fell three old biros, the key of the clock, a sixpenny piece, four paper clips, a stub of red crayon and a very surprised spider.

'Sorry!' said Hob, but the spider had already run away up the curtain.

Hob picked up the crayon.

'It's not what it ought to be, but it might just do,' he said.

He held it up close by the fireplace and wrote on the air with it. Miss Minkin was very interested.

Then Hob pushed at the air, first with both hands and then with his shoulder.

'Any luck?' asked Miss Minkin.

'No, it's still as stiff as a plank,' said Hob, 'Oaktree charcoal is what we must have or it won't work, but where are we to get such a thing in this day and age? The charcoal burners haven't been here for fifty years or more.' He shook his head. Then he sniffed the air.

'Talking of charcoal, what's been happening here?' he said.

'They cooked outside in the garden,' said Miss Minkin. 'They said it was a barbecue – that's what you can smell.'

'It reminds me of the ox-roast they had when the old squire's daughter got married,' said Hob. 'I remember it well! There was plenty for all and the beer flowed like water.'

'It was most inconvenient,' said Miss Minkin, 'I hadn't been asleep very long.'

Hob scratched his head. 'Let's go and look,' he said, 'we might find what we need out there.'

They slipped out through the cat flap and Miss Minkin showed Hob the barbecue. He jumped up onto the rim and peered in. He shook his head.

'There's nothing here but ash,' he said, 'not a sliver of good charcoal left anywhere. What's to do?'

Miss Minkin did not know.

Hob looked up at the night sky, where a sickle moon swung. He pointed and said, 'Look yonder!'

High above the weathercock on the barn, a shower of shooting stars fell through the night, dropping in bright arcs across the sky. The air was hushed, and the world seemed to stand still, as if it was waiting for something to happen.

Miss Minkin gasped. 'What does it mean?'

'Falling stars and a new moon on Midsummer Eve!' said Hob, 'The magic's up! Let's look for a star and make a wish.'

They looked up. Hob saw the first star fall, and he closed his eyes and wished hard. Then Miss Minkin saw two stars fall together, so she closed her eyes and had two wishes, although she did not mention it at the time.

'What was that?' said Hob.

They pricked up their ears and listened. Miss Minkin had just begun to say 'there's noth -' when Hob held up his hand.

'Hush!'

The air was full of murmuring and rustling, as if the wind had stirred the leaves in a great forest. Branching shadows fell across the farmyard and the house.

Miss Minkin's fur stood on end. She whispered, 'Do you believe in ghosts, Hob?'

'I won't say as I do, and I won't say as I don't,' said Hob, 'but I believe that on a night like this, all manner of things can happen.'

'For example?' asked Miss Minkin in a shaky little voice.

'For example, time can play tricks. Sometimes it stands still, and sometimes it runs backwards,' said Hob, 'and I think that's what it's doing now.'

Miss Minkin felt a little giddy, and sat down. Hob pointed at the shadows, 'Those are the old trees,' he said. 'It's Wych Wood. I remember when it was a mighty forest hereabouts; it spread across the Downs for miles. There were deer living there, and dangerous places in it where wild boar built their lairs. Nowadays, over yonder, it's nothing but houses and there are only a few trees left, round the pond.'

'I don't like the sound of wild boar in the least,' said Miss Minkin.

'Oh, they haven't been seen round here for many a long year,' said Hob.

'Mind you, neither has Wych Wood. The houses are built where great oaks and beeches once stood. You could see halfway to France from the tops of some of those trees; I've been up there myself. Now chimneys grow where the squirrels nested, and there are fences where the old forest tracks used to be. I don't suppose anybody could find them now, except maybe on a magical night like this.'

Miss Minkin's ears had twitched at the mention of nests.

'Are the squirrels there now, my dear, do you think?' she said.

'Most likely,' said Hob, 'wherever there's trees there's generally squirrels.'

'I SHOULD like to see where they live,' said Miss Minkin thoughtfully. 'It' a fine night; we could go for a stroll by the pond and see what we can see. What do you think of that?'

'Right you are!' said Hob. 'The moon's as thin as an elf's eyelid and the evening star is up. It's a grand time for a walk. Let's be off then, shall we?'

...

They stepped across the cobbles in the yard, slipped under the fence, and made for the bridge over the ghyll. Up the path on the other side was the road to the Wychwood estate. The rows of neat houses were in darkness.

'All abed,' said Hob.

As they approached the first garden fence, the night closed round them like a soft shawl. The roofs and the treetops beyond were silvery in the starlight, but the ground was in deep shadow. All the birds had gone to roost and the world was hushed.

'There IS something strange in the air tonight,' said Hob, 'I can feel it in my beard.'

'My whiskers are tingling too,' said Miss Minkin, 'keep close, dear Hob.'

They huddled together, peering round about, caught halfway between nervousness and excitement. Then, 'Look up yonder!' said Hob. The rooftops disappeared into the branching shadows. The whispering in the air like the rustling of leaves grew louder, but there was no wind.

'Listen!' squeaked Miss Minkin, 'something's coming! Help! Is it a wild boar?'

She crouched down flat to the earth. Hob cocked one ear.

'It sounds like wheels,' he said, 'look there!'

Through a break in the shadowy trees, a covered cart came trundling towards them. It passed quite close, and went on its way through a garden fence and a potting shed, following an invisible track. It bent not a single blade of grass; it left no wheeltracks. A tall man in a battered hat and a long black coat led the horse. Neither man nor horse left so much as a footprint. A woman rode in the cart, and a sleek black cat. The fur on Miss Minkin's neck rose and the tip of her tail began to twitch.

'Barley Puddock!' said Hob.

Miss Minkin gave him a long green stare. 'Speak English, please!' she said, crossly.

'It is English. It's Barley Puddock the charcoal burner and his wife Janetta,' said Hob. 'I haven't seen them since – ooh, the winter of forty seven, if I remember it right. Same old cat too - Wilf, he's called. I wonder what's brought them here?'

'Let's creep along behind them,' said Miss Minkin, 'and find out where they're going. I'm something of an expert at silent prowling. I bet even that cat won't know we're here.'

Hob nodded his head. 'Right enough,' he said, 'he won't know you from a nettle stalk. Come on.'

The two friends slipped along behind the cart, in and out of the shadows.

...

The cart stopped in a clearing, by a froggy pond. Hob and Miss Minkin crept under a bramble bush. Wilf jumped out of the cart. He washed his paws and chased a fly. Janetta built a fire for a brew of tea. Barley settled the horse. He took off his battered hat and hung it on a branch. The night air did not stir it, the thin branch did not bend. Hob and Miss Minkin watched from under the bramble bush.

At the edge of the clearing were shadowy stacks of wood. Barley looked, touched, weighed the pieces of wood in his hands. Ash and beech, chestnut and sycamore, and oak.

Barley and Janetta set about clearing a big circle of ground, sweeping up dead grass, beech mast and fallen leaves.

'They're making a hearth,' said Hob.

Wilf sat on a tree stump and glared at the frogs. The frogs took no notice. Barley played the mouth organ, and a strange old tune hopped and skittered through the trees.

Janetta danced round and round in her big boots, carefully stamping the earth flat. Barley drove a stake into the middle. He licked a finger and held it high in the air.

'Wind from the East,' he said.

They put up a canvas windscreen. They filled buckets with water from the pond and set them round and about. Nobody heard and nobody saw, except Miss Minkin and Hob.

Wilf prowled round the froggy pond and looked under bushes, but he had no luck at all. He passed within a whisper of the bramble bush. Miss Minkin arched her back and growled, but Wilf went on his silent way as if he had not heard.

'Hush my dear,' said Hob, 'he is only the shadow of a cat.'

• • •

Barley and Janetta stacked the wood up neatly in a big mound, with a chimney hole down through the middle. They covered it with turf, grassy side inwards. They smoothed and smoothed the turf cover until there was not a crack or a thin place in it anywhere for the wind to creep in.

Barley looked at the sky and Janetta tasted the wind again. The air was soft and still. Barley dropped glowing coals down the chimney hole, then covered the top and sealed it up. Smoke billowed out, first from the bottom of the mound, then towards the top. Then it died away. The watching and waiting began, under the stars.

Soon the air above the mound began to ripple and dance. A small blue-white cloud formed.

'That's the lait,' whispered Hob. 'That's good. It means there's no air getting in, so the wood won't burn.'

Miss Minkin was puzzled. 'Aren't they trying to burn it?' she asked.

'No,' said Hob, 'they're trying to bake it.'

Miss Minkin gazed at the mound and thought hard. Then she said, 'Oh, I see. It's an oven, not a bonfire.'

Hob smiled at her. 'How quickly you understand things, my dear.'

Miss Minkin looked at him sideways and remarked that speed of thought was natural in a cat.

• • •

From time to time, Janetta walked round the mound, looking and listening. All was quiet, all was well. From time to time she tasted the wind. Wilf fell asleep by the pond.

As Hob and Miss Minkin watched, hour by hour by hour, the mound was shrinking. Soon, it was only half as big as when it began. Time drifted on. The silent watchers did not know if they had been under the bramble a minute, or a day, or three. Then Miss Minkin saw Wilf wake, stretch and look up as the squirrels began to scamper and scold, high in the trees.

The work was done. As the mound cooled down, its hazy cap vanished in the still air. Barley and Janetta broke the baked turf cover. Fine black dust billowed over them as they sorted the charcoal. All the shapes and branches of the twigs could still be seen in it, like sooty fossils.

More dark dust covered Barley and Janetta as they sifted and sorted, until they were no more than shadows in the shadows. The dust drifted through the silent forest, covering it, hiding it from sight, drifting on the wind until everything was as black as the darkest night.

• • •

A fly buzzed round Miss Minkin's head. Her left ear twitched. The fly buzzed closer. Miss Minkin woke up with an angry 'Yow!' and waved her fists at the buzzing beast. It flew away. She looked around, and was very surprised to find herself under a rose bush in a neat little garden. The sun was just coming up, and next to her, Hob stretched and yawned behind his beard. A row of red-hatted gnomes seemed to be staring at them from across the lawn.

'Riff-raff!' said Hob. Miss Minkin snarled and spat. The gnomes stared on.

'Take no notice of them, my dear,' said Miss Minkin. She got up, shook herself, and looked around. There was not a tree in sight. Of Barley, Janetta and Wilf there was no sign, but by Hob's left foot was a long black knobbly twig. He picked it up.

'Oaktree charcoal!' he said. 'Thank you kindly,' he called to the empty air.

'We weren't dreaming, then?' asked Miss Minkin.

'We were visiting the long-ago, I reckon,' said Hob, 'but it's time to be homealong now. Folks will be about soon, and I don't want to be seen.'

'No, indeed,' said Miss Minkin.

They slipped through a hole in the fence and away. Nobody saw them go, and nobody saw them creep in through the cat flap at Ghyllside Farm. Hob wrote his easing runes on the air with the charcoal twig, and pushed. The invisible door swung open sweetly.

'That's my wish come true!' he said, and Miss Minkin said, 'Mine too, dear Hob.'

Footsteps sounded upstairs, and Hob disappeared. When the family came downstairs,

Miss Minkin had washed and was waiting for her breakfast, and Hob was under the hearthstone out of sight and sound.

Jenny put down a dish of nice minced chicken. Miss Minkin licked her pink lips.

'Mmm, that's wish number two!' she said, under her breath.

'I'll just open this window,' said Jenny, 'how that smell of charcoal does linger!'

Miss Minkin winked a thoughtful green eye at no-one in particular.

Carnival

4: Carnival

On a bright Autumn day, Miss Minkin was making her morning rounds of Ghyllside Farm. First she prowled round the hayrick, sniffing for mice. The mice were snuggled up deep in the middle of the stack and did not want to come out to play. Miss Minkin growled and lashed her tail. She stared hard at the hay and patted the stack with her paw, but the mice stayed put. After a while, Miss Minkin gave it up and went to inspect the barn. Not a single rat or spider was to be seen. It was a very disappointing morning. Once she had counted the sheep and glared at the hens, she thought she might as well go in for breakfast. She was just passing the tractor shed when her nose began to itch and she sneezed.

'Bless me!' said Miss Minkin, 'I hope I haven't caught a cold!'

She sneezed again. 'Bless me twice.'

She hurried indoors and spent the day in the warm, on a particularly soft cushion, in case she was coming down with something.

By the evening, after a nice fish supper, she was feeling very well again and looking forward to a visit from Hob.

• • •

That night, it was quite late before the family went to bed and left the house in peace. The children were excited and restless. Jenny was stitching long pieces of black cloth together with the sewing machine, and getting cross when the thread broke. Visitors came and went, bustling back and forth between the house and the tractor shed. They kept on leaving the house door open so that Miss Minkin was in a draft. What on earth were they up to? What was going on? She was very glad when they all went home.

The family clumped upstairs at last. Soon after they had gone, Hob slipped out of the shadows behind the fire-irons.

'Good evening my dear, what's the news?' he said.

'You might well ask!' said Miss Minkin, 'Peace was not to be had in house nor yard today, and there's something sneezy in the tractor shed.'

‘I’m very sorry to hear it,’ said Hob, ‘shall I play a soothing little tune on me fiddle?’

‘Please do,’ purred Miss Minkin, and Hob played a melody so soft and sweet it would have calmed the nerves of a raging tiger, never mind a nice old tabby cat. While he was playing, a big yellow September moon swung across the sky and poured light in through a gap in the curtains. It made a golden path across the floor. Hob pointed to it with his fiddle bow.

‘Look there!’ he whispered.

Miss Minkin’s green eyes followed the line of the moonbeam. Where it met the kitchen wall, there was a dark shadow on the floor like the outline of a door.

‘I’ve never noticed that before!’ said Miss Minkin, ‘what ever can it be?’

‘It’s a hideyhole,’ said Hob, ‘leastways, it was, once upon a day. It’s been blocked up for years and years. I’d almost forgotten it was there until the moon reminded me.’

‘Oh?’ said Miss Minkin. She made herself comfortable. She felt sure there was a story coming on. Hob lit his pipe and perched on a firedog.

'A long time ago, before your dear great-great-grandmother was even a kitten,' he said, 'there was once a dangerous time at Ghyllside Farm.'

Miss Minkin opened her green eyes very wide. 'Dangerous?'

'Aye,' said Hob, 'there were smugglers all along the Sussex coast in those days, and on many a dark night there'd be folk slipping through the shadows, with baccy and brandy and French lace. If the excise men were on to 'em, they would have to find a place to hide the stuff where t'wouldn't be found. Sometimes they came to the farms at dead of night and stashed the stuff in a barn, or an attic or cellar, or in the middle of a haystack maybe, and the folk wouldn't know it was there - until the gang came back for it. Some of them were desperate fellows, too. The Alfriston gang was as nasty a bunch of cut-throats as ever I saw.'

Miss Minkin gave a little scream, 'As ever you saw! Don't tell me they came here!'

'Aye, they did, though,' said Hob. 'One night, I heard someone creeping about up here after the family had long gone to bed, so I came up for a look-see. There were three of 'em; two over by the trap door, and one by the stairs keeping lookout, with a pistol in his hand.'

Miss Minkin gasped. 'Whatever did you do?'

Hob chuckled. 'I did a switching spell. The farmer's old boots were warming by the hearth, so I switched 'em with the stuff the gang had just hidden in the cellar. They closed the trap door and turned to creep away, and there were all the boxes and barrels sitting by the hearth. 'What!' says one, 'you left some behind, you great fool! Look there!'

'Not I!' says the other, 'I stowed every last bit of it.'

'Rot ye for a lazy mumper!' he said (and a lot more besides), 'get and do the job properly this time. I'm a-watching you, mind!'

So they lifted the trap door and stowed all the stuff down there once more, and as soon as they'd finished, I switched it all back again.

'What! There's witchcraft here!' says one, 'It's the devil hisself!' says the other, and they're all swearing and falling over each other to get out of the door. They went across the fields like long dogs, I can tell you. I laughed until I pretty near cried. Then I spirited all the stuff deep down under the potato clamp in case the Excise Men came snooping.'

'Oh well done my dear!' purred Miss Minkin, 'but what about the poor farmer's boots? Did he ever find them again?'

'Of course he did,' said Hob, 'they were by the hearth. The switching spell only lasts until morning. Listen.'

He waved his arms and began to chant:

'For this night
'Til morning's light
Get you to the cellar space;
What is there will take your place.'

When Hob finished, one hand was pointing at the clock on the mantelpiece. There was a fizzing and a whooshing and a small flash of lightning, and the clock vanished.

'Oh Lawks! I didn't mean to do that,' said Hob.

Where the clock had been was an old battered pewter pot all covered in cobwebs. Miss Minkin gasped.

'What is it?'

Hob went to take a closer look.

'I think it's an ale-pot,' he said, 'and there's writing on it.'

'Oh, read it out, dear Hob, do! It might be a secret message!' cried Miss Minkin.

Hob blew some of the cobwebs off.

'It says, 'Leave'n be. T'ain't your'n.' C.H. A.D.1742' he said.

'Oh, how exciting! Is that Old French?'

'More like Old Sussex. It's someone who didn't want their ale pinched, I reckon.' Hob scratched his beard. 'Must've been old Clem Hemsley. Mighty fond of his ale, he was - and didn't like sharing it!'

A spider ran out of the ale-pot and disappeared into the dark behind the calendar.

Miss Minkin bounded towards the fireplace and crouched low. Her green eyes glared. She lashed her tail and growled.

'Come out!' she spat.

'No thanks,' said a spidery little voice.

'Leave mother spider be, my dear,' said Hob, 'she won't do any harm, and she'll be back in the cellar by morning.'

'I hope so,' said the spidery voice.

Miss Minkin said nothing more, but the tip of her tail went on twitching for a while.

All the excitement had made them thirsty, so they drank the dish of cream. Hob sipped from his silver thimble and Miss Minkin lapped straight from the dish. When she had cleaned her whiskers, she said,

'But what happened then?'

'Let me see,' said Hob, 'the Alfriston gang ran off so fast their feet left scorch marks across the yard.'

'Really?' said Miss Minkin.

'Well, nearly,' said Hob, 'in any case, they never came back.'

'But what about their things?' said Miss Minkin, 'didn't the farmer find them?'

Hob thought for a long moment. He scratched his beard and puffed his pipe.

'As far as I know, he never did find them,' he said at last, 'I think they must be still under the potato clamp.'

Miss Minkin's tabby ears pricked up. She jumped to her feet and ran to the door. 'Come on!' she said.

Out through the catflap she went, with Hob close behind. The huge golden moon sailed over the housetop, making deep shadows over the yard.

Hob looked carefully all around. He shook his head.

'It's all changed,' he said, 'I'm blessed if I can remember where the potato clamp used to be.'

'Oh, purrLEASE try, dear Hob,' said Miss Minkin, 'I should so like to see the smuggler's hoard - especially the fine French lace.'

Hob swivelled slowly round, and finally he pointed to the tractor shed.

'There!' he said, 'the shed's on top of it. That's what muddled me up.'

They ran towards the tractor shed, but when they got close to it, they both began to sneeze and SNEEZE.

'Bless me!' said Hob, 'that's strong stuff, what ever it is, but what's it doing here?'

'I meant to tell you about it,' said Miss Minkin, 'is it some kind of magic?'

'It doesn't feel like magic,' said Hob, 'more like some human mischief. I'll cover it with scent-blanket, shall I? That should fix it. What flavour would you like?'

'Well, mice is nice,' said Miss Minkin, 'or herring.'

Hob scratched his beard. 'Whatever you like, my dear,' he said, 'but you realise all the other cats will smell it too? It'll fetch 'em here in droves.'

'What!' spluttered Miss Minkin, 'not that mincing Siamese from the big house? Not the hairy black tom from over the ghyll?'

'ALL of them,' said Hob.

'Roast chicken, then?' said Miss Minkin hopefully.

'That'll fetch the dogs, too,' said Hob.

Miss Minkin sighed. 'All right, you choose,' she said, 'but please make it something nice.'

Hob smiled. 'I'll do that all right, don't you fret. He took out his pipe and lit it. He waved it in the air and made a blanket of smoke-rings. Then he sang:

'Sweet oils of Araby, spices of Africa,
Essence of catnip (sweeter than roses),
Cover the mischief, smother the sneezing,
Perfume the air and comfort our noses.'

Miss Minkin's green eyes misted over.

'Pure poetry!' she sighed, 'and catnip too - my other favourite!'

'I'm quite partial to it myself!' said Hob.

They crept towards the shed, under the blanket of sweet smells. Neither of them sneezed again. They squeezed into the shed under the ricketty door, and peered round in the gloom.

'I'm pretty sure this is the place,' said Hob, 'I'll try a fetching spell.'

He held out his arms, closed his eyes and chanted;

'Once under earth I bade you stay;
The binding spell I now UNSAY!'

The earth floor of the shed began to quiver and heave. Miss Minkin gave a little scream and jumped up on a pile of long sticks in the corner. Up through the floor came three fat little barrels and two boxes. Miss Minkin waited a second to make sure there were no more earthquakes, and then jumped off the pile of sticks. She sniffed at the boxes.

'Can you open them please, dear Hob?'

Hob pointed to the boxes. 'Open ye!' he commanded.

The boxes sprang open. Inside were mouldy scraps of what was once fine French lace, and rotten shreds of what was once good tobacco.

'Oh no!' said a disappointed Miss Minkin.

'Close ye!' said a disappointed Hob, and the boxes closed.

Hob picked up one of the barrels and shook it. Then the next. Then the third.

'Empty!' he said gloomily. 'It's a crying shame. Evaporated, I reckon. Buried too long.'

Hob sighed. 'Come on my dear,' he said, 'there's no use in moping here, let's go back into the warm.'

As they crossed the yard, the stars were growing pale and the moon was sinking behind the Downs.

'Let's hurry,' said Miss Minkin, 'the dew is coming up and it will flatten my fur.'

'By all means,' said Hob, 'it'll be light soon and I must be away. After you through the cat flap, my dear.'

While it was still quite dark, Hob slipped away to his secret place under the hearthstone and Miss Minkin settled down for a short snooze after the excitements of the night. By and by, Jenny came down the stairs. She pointed to the mantelpiece and gave a little shriek.

'Either I've gone mad or I'm still asleep and dreaming,' she said. 'What's that dusty old pot doing there? And where's the clock gone to?'

Miss Minkin was wide awake now. She remembered Hob's switching spell and felt rather hot and pink under her tabby fur.

Jenny ran to the window and pulled back the curtain. As the morning light poured in, there was a fizzing and a whooshing and a small flash of lightning, and Hob's switching spell was broken. The old pewter pot went back to the cellar, and the clock was in its usual place on the mantelpiece.

'Ooh! Whatever was that?' gasped poor Jenny. She gazed frantically round the room. She saw the clock. She blinked twice and rubbed her eyes. She sat down on a chair, heavily. Womp! Miss Minkin watched her with alarm.

'Either I am going off my head or it was those pickled onions I ate last night,' said Jenny to herself. 'I thought they tasted funny. Or perhaps I should get my eyes tested. I could have sworn my clock wasn't there when I first looked.'

Miss Minkin went to her and purred very nicely. She rubbed Jenny's legs with her soft head.

'Dear old cat,' said Jenny, stroking Miss Minkin's tabby fur, 'let's get on with the day. Breakfast?'

Miss Minkin purred louder.

The children were even more excited that day. They ran about waving wooden pistols and shouting, 'In the name of the King!' until Miss Minkin couldn't bear it any more. She took herself off to the airing cupboard for some peace and quiet. It was early evening before she ventured back into the farm kitchen. The house door was open again, and all kinds of strange people were coming and going.

'Really!' said Miss Minkin to herself, 'they might have some consideration for others. There's a draft! What on earth is going on now?'

She went to the door and peered out. There were lights in the tractor shed, and the farmer was just coming out with his arms full of the long sticks. He was dressed in a dark cloak and black hat, and there was soot on his face.

'Torches!' he shouted, then he sneezed.

'Mind yourself, Miss Minkin,' said Jenny from behind, 'you'll get trodden on there. Just you keep indoors while we get all the torches out - smelly old things; they'll give you the sneezlums.'

Miss Minkin looked up. Jenny's face was blackened too. Then two black-faced children ran by, yelling, 'I'm a smuggler bold from the days of old! Can we carry a torch, Dad? Dad, can we?'

'Wait and see,' said their father, 'you could help get the stuff out of the shed.'

Suddenly, Miss Minkin understood. Fancy dress costumes, torches, the first moon of September - it was bonfire and carnival time! She sprang up onto the windowsill where she could watch the fun and keep out of the way of stomping feet. The children ran out of the tractor shed carrying the barrels and boxes.

'Look at this stuff!' they shouted. 'It's great! It looks like a real smuggler's hoard! Can we carry it in the procession?'

Miss Minkin smiled to herself. Just then she felt something brush her front paw. It was Hob, although if she hadn't known she might have thought he was just a shadow on the curtain.

'I heard the commotion and came up early,' he said, 'I do love carnival.'

'Me too!' said Miss Minkin, 'shall we go along?'

'We shall indeed!' said Hob.

The farmer appeared with a flaming piece of wood, and everyone crowded round to have their torches lit.

'Watch,' said Hob from the shadows in the curtains. He pointed at the torches and muttered something Miss Minkin could not quite hear.

Suddenly there were bursts of bright flames, orange and rose and gold. Curling trails of blue and green smoke drifted off into the air. Everyone gasped.

'They're the loveliest thing I've ever seen,' said Jenny.

'I reckon they are, too!' beamed the farmer. 'It must be some new kind of stuff they've put on them. Whatever it is, it's a marvel. It's a show all on its own, that is.'

As they watched, glowing bubbles floated up from amongst the flames. They hovered in the air a moment and then popped, filling the air with coloured sparks.

'Oooh! Aaah!'

The farmer lifted his torch high and marched round with it, grinning.

'Pretty as a posy!' he said, 'and we've got fifty of 'em! If we don't win first prize tonight, I'll eat my Sunday hat! None of the others will have torches like ours – they're magic!'

Miss Minkin opened her beautiful green eyes very wide.

'Yes indeed,' she murmured.

• • •

When everyone had left the house, Hob and Miss Minkin crept out into the yard and watched from a shadowy corner as the procession of smugglers and excise men formed up. The wonderful torches lit up the evening sky with their rainbow flames and sparks as the folk marched off up the lane, singing a smuggler's song. Behind them, keeping out of sight under the overhanging grass at the lane edge, trotted two small figures, one on two legs and the other on four. Nobody noticed them at all.

'I DO love the bonfire and carnival,' said Miss Minkin, 'I hope the fireworks are good.'

'Oh, they will be!' said Hob.

Hallowe'en

5: Halloween

It was late October. Fallen leaves covered the ground at Ghyllside Farm, crisp and frosty in the early mornings. Miss Minkin had to lift her paws and shake them very often when she was out walking, so she stayed indoors by the fire as much as she could. The evenings were drawing in and the nights were colder too. Miss Minkin grew a fluffy winter coat, and Hob put on his warm moleskin jerkin and an extra pair of socks. One evening, he appeared from the shadows behind the fire-irons and said,

'Is it safe? Have they gone to bed? The porch light is still on.'

'I think they must be in bed,' said Miss Minkin, 'I was having a little nap after supper, and when I woke up the house was quiet. They must have gone up early.'

'It's getting chilly. I expect they wanted their warm beds,' said Hob. 'Mind you, winters are not what they were. I remember when the sea froze over at Newhaven and the fishing boats couldn't get out for weeks.'

'How perfectly dreadful,' murmured Miss Minkin.

'Then there was the time the River Thames in London was frozen from bank to bank. People skated on it and built a great fire on the ice and roasted an ox.'

Miss Minkin shivered at the thought of all that nasty ice on her beautiful tabby paws, and tucked them under her white bib to keep them warm.

'Please talk about something else,' she begged, 'and do help yourself to cream.'

'Thank you kindly,' said Hob, 'but after you, my dear.'

Miss Minkin purred and lapped the cream with her dainty pink tongue, then Hob dipped his silver thimble in and had his turn.

When they had almost finished the cream, they sang a round of 'Great Tom.' They had been practising it for ages, and tonight they got it perfectly right for the first time. They were quite pleased with themselves.

• • •

Hob and Miss Minkin were very snug by the embers of the fire. The fireglow cast deep flickering shadows in the corners of the kitchen. Hob liked watching the shadows dance, but Miss Minkin sat with her back to them. She had pounced on one once, thinking it was a giant mouse, and had given her paw a nasty knock on the skirting board.

'Shadows are horrid things,' said Miss Minkin.

'Are you frightened of them?' asked Hob.

Miss Minkin was indignant. 'Frightened of shadows?' she said, 'I, who come from a long line of fierce hunters? I'll have you know my nerves are like steel.'

'I'm sorry my dear,' said Hob, humbly, 'I didn't mean to, upset you. I know you are very brave indeed. A warrior among cats!'

'Yes,' said Miss Minkin, 'you need have no fear while I'm around to protect you.'

Hob was a little put out at that.

'Fear?' he said, 'I don't know the meaning of the word! My ancestors fought with dragons as big as mountains, don't forget!'

There was silence for a while, but they did not like to quarrel, and soon Miss Minkin said, 'Have a little more cream, my dear,' and Hob said, 'after you, my dear,' and they were comfortable again.

As the fire died, the shadows leaped and danced round the walls, and Hob said they put him in mind of ghostly tales of long ago. He lit his pipe, took a thimbleful of cream, and told story after story of ghouls and boggarts, phantoms and witches. Some of the stories were quite funny, like the one about the haunted hot water bottle, which jumped out of bed on moonlit nights and hopped round the bedroom. But when Hob started on The Ghostly Dog of Blackness Lane, who had eyes like flaming coals and crept up behind people on silent paws to howl in their ears, Miss Minkin felt the hair on the back of her neck begin to rise. Suddenly she jumped up. Hob said, 'What's that?' An eerie, shrieking sound tore round the house and down the chimney. It was a hard, cold wind, full of sleet, gusting across the night and howling, Whooo-ooo-ooh!

Miss Minkin shivered and drew closer to the fire. The wind seemed to find every crack and cranny in the old farmhouse. Doors banged shut, doors flew open, the fire-irons rattled and the window curtains flapped. Dead leaves and icy drops of sleet battered against the windows, rat-a-tat-a-tat, like someone knocking on the glass.

'It sounds like someone or something trying to get in!' said Miss Minkin through chattering teeth.

'It's only the w-w-wind,' said Hob, but even he did not sound too sure. The stories of ghouls and ghostly hounds were still fresh in his mind. There was a flapping noise above his head.

'Oh, what's that?' he squeaked, but it was only the wind ruffling the pages of Jenny's calendar on the wall. Hob stared at the red ring round the date: October 31st.

'Oh no!' he said.

'What's the matter?' asked Miss Minkin.

'It's Halloween! The night when witches and spooks are out and about and making mischief!' said Hob.

Miss Minkin was a little worried for a moment, but then she had an idea.

'Don't you know any spells against spooks?' she asked.

'Y-yes,' stammered Hob, 'but I can't seem to think of any at the m-m-moment.'

There was another howl from the wind and another loud tattoo on the window. Miss Minkin jumped up.

'I think I'd feel safer under the sofa!' she said, and she dived beneath it, much to the surprise of a small black beetle who was minding his own business under there. Miss Minkin, whose nerves were in rags, hissed at him and he scuttled away under the skirting board, very fast. Then she curled up and put her paws over her eyes.

...

When Miss Minkin felt brave enough to move her paws and open her eyes, she looked round. Where was Hob? He wasn't under the sofa with her! She peeped out. He was not on the hearth either! What if there really were spooks, and they'd got him? At first, she could not think what to do, but then she remembered that she came from a long line of fierce hunters. She crouched low and thrashed her tail from side to side. She fluffed her fur up, and her eyes flashed green and tigerish. She unsheathed her claws and began to growl loud enough to frighten anything.

'Whatever is the matter?' said Hob.

He bent down and peered under the sofa at the fierce hunter.

'It's all right, you can come out now,' he said.

Miss Minkin stopped growling and put her claws away. She came out.

'I'm so glad you're safe,' she said, 'where were you?'

'I was putting a holding spell on the doors and windows,' he said, 'just in case something tries to get in. You never know on a night like this.'

'Did you see anything?' asked Miss Minkin anxiously.

'No, and it's just as well,' he said, 'because I still can't remember any spells against spooks, but then I thought of holding the doors and windows fast. We should be all right now. Let's have some music to cheer ourselves up.'

'Something jolly, please,' said Miss Minkin.

Hob tuned his fiddle and played a jig. Then Miss Minkin recited one of her favourite poems, The Naming of Cats, which was very stirring. The wind had dropped and all was quiet around the house.

'I feel much better now,' said Hob.

'So do I,' Miss Minkin agreed, 'do you think there really were ghosts and ghouls outside?'

Hob hung his head. 'No,' he said, 'I'm pretty sure we were just being silly, and it was only the wind. No more ghost stories for us, my dear – they're bad for our nerves. Let's play a nice game of I Spy instead.

...

They had several good rounds of I Spy. Miss Minkin guessed CD (cream dish) and MH (mouse hole) and Hob guessed E (embers) and FI (fire irons).

'This is too easy!' he said. When it was his turn again, he scratched his head and thought hard. He looked up at the window.

'I've got it!' he said, 'you'll never guess this one – GM.'

Try as she might, Miss Minkin could not guess it, and she was a champion I Spy player. Finally, she had to give in. Hob pointed to a small gap in the window curtains and said 'Gibbous moon!'

'Whatever is that?' asked Miss Minkin, 'I've never heard of such a thing!'

'Come and look,' said Hob, and he hopped up onto the windowsill.

Miss Minkin sprang up beside him. He held the curtain back, and there was a pale moon, wreathed in mist, high above them.

'It's a funny shape,' said Miss Minkin, 'like a big white eye. I don't think I like it much.'

'It's just a bit more than three-quarters full,' said Hob, 'gibbous is what it's called when it's that shape.'

'You know so much, my dear!' said Miss Minkin, admiringly.

Hob grinned. 'It comes of living so long,' he said.

They sat on the windowsill and watched the moon sailing along in the misty sky. Now that the wind had dropped, the night was very still, and the ground was blanketed in a grey fog, which hung from the trees in long wispy rags. The porch light shone across the yard on shapes made strange by the mist.

'What's that horrible bulgy-looking lump over there?' asked Miss Minkin.

Hob peered through the glass as best he could.

'I think it's only the wood pile,' he said, 'but I'm not sure. What's that long snakey thing?'

'Oh, I don't know,' said Miss Minkin, 'it could be Jenny's washing pole, or it could be something else! It's not moving, is it? Is it coming this way?'

'Now, my dear, we mustn't start getting nervous again,' said Hob, 'there's nothing out there but a bit of autumn mist. Aaarghh!'

He jumped to his feet and pointed to the window pane. Miss Minkin's fur stood right upon end at what she saw. A ghastly grinning orange head without a body was floating across the yard. Its horrible eyes flickered. Behind it was a procession of dreadful spooks and ghouls; a glowing green skeleton, a witch with long purple hair, a ghost in flowing white robes and a small red devil with a pitchfork and long tail. They were jigging up and down and chanting something Hob and Miss Minkin couldn't quite hear. Then, 'Whooo-oo-ooh!' They heard that, all right.

'Oh, Hob dear, please remember the spell!' quavered Miss Minkin.

'I... I c-c-can't! My brain is a jelly! It's... Terrible – no, Horrible...no...Oh, help!'

The dreadful procession came closer. They were almost across the yard now. The small red devil tripped over his tail and said, 'Bother!'

'Got it!' shouted Hob,

'Bothersome sprites and ghouls begone!
Evil night-frighteners leave us alone!
Witches and warlocks get you home!
With all your wicked japes be done!'

He waved his arms three times round in the air. Nothing happened. The spooks were still there, and they were coming up the path! Hob gabbled the spell again, louder, and waved his arms like windmills. Still the spooks came on. They were almost at the door!

'It hasn't worked!' wailed Miss Minkin, 'oh, please do SOMETHING!'

'I don't understand it,' said Hob, 'it's a very good spell against evil. Never failed before. I'll try doubling the holding spell.'

'Hold fast, bolt and lock,
Open not to those who knock.
Keep tight, clasp and pin,
Let no creature out or in!'

The spooks had reached the front door. The green skeleton took hold of the door handle and rattled it.

'How long does your spell last?' quivered Miss Minkin.

'I don't rightly know,' shivered Hob, 'I haven't used it these three hundred years. Save yourself, my dear – run!'

• • •

In less than the twinkling of an eye, Miss Minkin was upstairs in the darkest corner of the airing cupboard with her paws over her eyes, and Hob was deep under the hearthstone with his hat over his. They stayed like that for a long time, but by and by they stopped shivering with fright and their hearts stopped pounding. They listened and listened, but nothing came after them, and in the quiet darkness, each of them fell asleep at last.

In the morning, when Miss Minkin woke up she remembered the terrible events of the evening before.

It was a little while before she felt brave enough to peep round the door of the airing cupboard, but she was hungry, and in the end she thought she would just put her nose out to see what was happening. There was a noise from downstairs, but it was breakfasty rather than ghosty. Miss Minkin ventured out and crept down the stairs. She looked round the door of the kitchen. There on the table was a big orange pumpkin with a face cut in it. Propped against the wall were a broomstick and a pitchfork. On top of the pitchfork was a purple wig. Miss Minkin stood quite still in the doorway and looked at all the strange things.

'Put that dressing-up clutter away now, please,' said Jenny, 'we won't need it again until next year.'

'Oh, Mum!' said Ben, 'I want to wear my devil's costume to Ryan's party on Saturday.'

Miss Minkin sat down, looking thoughtful. She was wondering how to tell Hob, later.

Just then, Jenny's husband came in with some tools in his hand and said, 'It's a total mystery.

There's nothing wrong with that door now, and it was completely jammed last night. It must have been the rain.'

'Well,' said Jenny, 'you'd better keep your eye on it. I didn't enjoy climbing in through the coal-hole.'

'Serves them right!' said Miss Minkin to herself, 'people get up to some very silly tricks sometimes. They ought to know better.' Then she remembered breakfast and went to Jenny, purring very nicely.

Jenny bent down and stroked her.

'Hello Miss Minkin,' she said, 'where were you last night? Off somewhere having an adventure? Did you have a nice time?'

Miss Minkin stopped purring and gave Jenny a long sideways look.

The Christmas Presents

6: The Christmas Presents

The December moon swung high over Ghyllside Farm, bright as a promise and round as pudding. The first snow of winter lay crisp and white over the fields. The farm folk were all abed, snuggled down and fast asleep, dreaming of plumcake and presents. Down in the kitchen by the fire, Hob and Miss Minkin were toasting their toes. There was a smell of pine- needles in the air from the sparkling tree in the corner, and there were two large stockings hanging from the mantelpiece. The stockings belonged to the farm children, and had their names pinned on them: Ben and Susan. The children had hung them there before they went to bed. They had put a small glass of sherry and a plate with two mince pies on it, by the hearth.

'In case he's hungry,' said Susan.

Miss Minkin had watched all this with great interest, and told Hob about it later.

‘Who did she mean?’ asked Hob, ‘Nobody knows about me. Nobody has ever seen me.’

‘She must have made a mistake. She meant to say ‘she,’ said Miss Minkin, ‘she’s a good girl and she left the things for me, but you shall share them, my dear.’

‘Thank you, I’m sure!’ said Hob. They ate the spicy pies to the last crumb.

‘Very tasty!’ said Hob. Miss Minkin was not so sure. Then they sipped the sherry, but it made Miss Minkin cough a little so Hob kindly finished it up. He left a silver sixpence under the plate for good manners.

‘This is all very pleasant,’ he said, ‘It must be Christmas again, I suppose.’

‘Yes,’ said Miss Minkin, ‘Jenny has been charging round the kitchen boiling and baking and getting hot and cross. She even forgot my morning milk! I had to yowl to remind her, and then she slapped it down in a very grumpy manner. I kept well out of the way after that. I spent most of the day snoozing in the airing cupboard.’

‘Dear me, what a difficult day you’ve had!’ said Hob, ‘she shall find a frog in her shoe in the morning for being unkind.’

'Oh, please don't bother,' said Miss Minkin, 'she was sorry after and gave me all the bacon rind. I have forgiven her. Christmas is a trying time for her. I like it, though, on the whole. There is always plenty of leftover turkey.'

Hob puffed on his pipe.

'It's a merry time, right enough,' he said, 'I remember in the old days there was always a great deal of eating and drinking and dancing and wassailing. Neighbours went all round the houses and sang a song or two, and people gave them spiced ale and presents.'

Miss Minkin put her head on one side and thought for a while.

'I should like to have presents,' she said, 'I have a very sweet voice and you can play the fiddle pretty well. What do you think, my dear? Shall we go a-wassailing?'

'Indeed we shall!' said Hob, 'That is a fine idea. The neighbours will like to hear some good old Christmas music. It will cheer them up.'

Hob fetched his fiddle and a sack to bring all the presents home in. Miss Minkin washed her face and combed her ears. They slipped out through the cat flap into the snowy moonlit garden. Miss Minkin sniffed the air and said it was safe to be out. There was no smell of fox or badger. Hob looked up.

'A fine night indeed, but there's a nip in the air,' he said. He was wearing a stout green jacket and hat, and Miss Minkin had fluffed up her beautiful fur, so neither of them minded it much.

'Where to?' asked Hob.

'Let's try Berryman's Farm first,' said Miss Minkin, 'the farmer's wife is fond of me and they keep a very good larder.'

They set off across the round the henhouse, and ducked under the gate to Halfacre Field. Their footsteps crunched on the frosty grass. Only the moon saw them cross the wooden bridge over the murmuring ghyll and turn down the lane to Berryman's. Farmer Croft had just filled the coal scuttle and taken off his boots before going to bed. Miss Minkin cleared her throat and Hob tightened his fiddle bow.

'Ready!' he said, 'one, two, three!'

He played a good loud opening chord, and they began 'Ding Dong Merrily on High' with all their hearts.

Hardly had they sung the first line when a boot and three lumps of coal came flying through the farmhouse window. The boot sailed over their heads and lodged in the branches of a tree, and the lumps of coal fell right in front of their feet. They were quite surprised, but they remembered their manners and called out, 'Thank you! Merry Christmas!'

Hob looked up at the tree.

'What was that?' he said.

'I don't know, it sailed by so fast and high,' said Miss Minkin, but we must try to get it down. It's a present and the farmer will think it very rude if we leave it in the tree. He'll think we didn't want it.'

'True enough,' said Hob. Then he waved his fiddle bow three times round and pointed it at the tree.

'Come!' he said, and the boot came tumbling down at his feet. Hob scratched his head.

'I'm sure this is kindly meant,' he said, 'but one boot on its own is a strange sort of present. It will be heavy to carry home, and then what would we do with it?'

'We don't want to hurt his feelings,' said Miss Minkin, 'shall we hide it somewhere?'

They pushed the boot a long way behind the staddlestones, where nobody could see it. In the spring, a pair of mice moved in and raised a family of ten. They were very snug.

The farmer looked all over the yard for his boot the next morning, but it was well hidden. It was his good boot, too. It was the other one that had a hole in. He had to hop on one leg all over Christmas until the shops opened again.

...

Hob picked up the lumps of coal and put them in the sack. He covered them with straw for tidiness.

'This is very generous,' he said.

Miss Minkin would have helped him, but was afraid of blackening her beautiful paws. Hob said he didn't mind a bit of honest dirt.

'Where to now?' he said.

'The Bird and Hurdle, I think,' said Miss Minkin, 'they keep a good kitchen and I have done them some favours in the matter of rats.'

Off they went, over the crisp white fields, through the hedge and across the lane, to the back door of The Bird and Hurdle. The landlady, Peg Brewer, was already fast asleep and dreaming of Christmas pudding. Her husband Tom had stayed to lock up, and had just poured himself a last pot of Christmas ale before bedtime when Hob struck up on his fiddle and Miss Minkin began to sing at the top of her voice. She had not got much further than 'Silent Night, Ho –' when the door opened and the pot of ale came sailing out. Hob dropped the bow and caught it one-handed.

'Oh well done!' said Miss Minkin, 'how clever!'

'It's nearly full of good ale, too!' said Hob.

He put the pot of ale carefully in the sack, waved his fiddle bow three times round it and sang:

'Stay right side up,
Neither spill nor slop.'

And it didn't.

'This is more than kind of our good neighbours,' said Miss Minkin, 'I expect he remembered me and the rats and he wanted to say thank you.'

In the morning, Mr Brewer looked everywhere for his favourite pewter pot, but he never did find it.

...

'The sack's middling heavy now,' said Hob, 'shall we be getting home-along?'

'Yes,' said Miss Minkin, 'but let's call at Windlemoor as we go. It's on the way home, and the Missus has always had a soft spot for me.'

Hob shouldered the sack and off they went. The moon was beginning to set, and the stars were very bright as they went back down the lane towards Windlemoor. An owl swooped low over their heads on silent wings, and Hob wished it good night and good hunting.

• • •

At Windlemoor House, the whole day had been busy with Christmas preparations, and Mrs Biggins was still up and about with some last-minute jobs. The back door was open to let out the heat of the Christmas baking. Mrs Biggins was sorting out chunks of marrowbone for roasting in the morning when Hob and Miss Minkin came through the garden gate and up the path. They stopped outside the door and began 'O Come All Ye Faithful'. Mrs Biggins jumped, screamed and threw the chunks of marrowbone up in the air. They came bouncing out of the door like skittles, and Miss Minkin had to step smartly out of the way. Hob picked up the marrowbones and put them in the sack.

'Really, our neighbours are very good,' he said. He called out 'Merry Christmas!' but a gust of wind must have caught the door and made it slam shut.

In the morning, when Mr Biggins asked for the Christmas marrowbones, his wife gave him a very black look and told him he could have cold mutton and like it.Hob and Miss Minkin made their way home in the fading moonlight, under the Christmas stars. Hob stumped along with his fiddle in one hand and the sack over his shoulder. Miss Minkin watched where she was stepping and took care not to get her paws too snowy. They were very pleased with their night's work.

'Wassailing is a very good thing,' said Miss Minkin, 'I'm glad I thought of it.'

'Yes, my dear, the folk round here are very kind, although their manners are a little rough,' said Hob, 'In the olden days, if I remember rightly, they didn't throw the presents at people – but times change, I suppose.'

'Hurry along now, please,' said Miss Minkin, 'my fur is getting damp.'

• • •

The slipped quietly through the cat flap at Ghyllside Farm, and into the shadowy kitchen. It was late into the night, and the fire was dying. Hob and Miss Minkin were feeling a little chilly. Hob blew on the embers to make them glow, and piled on the straw and the three lumps of coal. He soon had a good blaze going, and he and Miss Minkin were warm and cosy once more. Then Hob took the pewter pot and put the ale to warm on the hearth. Last of all, he set the marrowbones to roast on the grate. While they were sizzling, he lit his pipe and blew several perfect smoke rings round the star on top of the Christmas tree. Miss Minkin washed her face and paws, ready for the feast.

'Merry Christmas!' she said as she eyed the sizzling marrowbones. Hob lifted the pewter pot, 'Wassail!'

They feasted and danced until morning began to light up the eastern sky, and had just nodded off to sleep when there was a noise of feet scrambling down the stairs, and the children came running in. Hob slipped into the shadows and was back under the hearthstone in no time at all. Miss Minkin opened one eye.

The children took the bulging stockings down and began to shout, 'I've got a doll!' 'He's given me a train!' 'Look, a chocolate mouse! A spinning top!'

They ran upstairs to tell their parents that Father Christmas had eaten the mince pies and drunk the sherry, and had left lots of marvellous presents in the stockings and two old bones and a pewter pot on the hearth.

Miss Minkin closed her eyes and settled down for a long Christmas Morning nap.

The End

Lightning Source UK Ltd.
Milton Keynes UK
UKOW06f0048110216

268103UK00001B/44/P